BIG
STONES
AND
ROX
BEE
TREE
MY
HOUSE
EEYORES
GLOOMY
PLACE
OWLS
HOUSE
MR SHEPARD HELPD

Based on the "Winnie the Pooh" works, by A.A. Milne and E.H. Shepard.
Published by Hachette Partworks Ltd
ISBN: 978-1-906965-55-6
Date of Printing: May 2011
Printed in Singapore
by Tien Wah Press

Disney
Winnie the Pooh

Disney
hachette

Deep in the Hundred-Acre Wood lived a boy named Christopher Robin and his stuffed bear, Winnie the Pooh. The two shared many adventures with their friends in this very special place.

One morning when Pooh awoke, his tummy was especially hungry for honey. When Pooh could not find any honey at home, he went outside in search of some.

First, Pooh went to Eeyore's house. But Eeyore didn't have any honey. Pooh noticed that Eeyore also didn't have any tail.

"I, Winnie the Pooh, will find your tail," he said. "And then I shall get some honey."

Just then, a voice came from a nearby tree.

"Chapter One: The Birth of a Genius," it began. "A breezy wind whiffed through the wood as I stood majestically atop the enormous tree..."

Pooh and Eeyore turned to listen to the tree, which sounded a lot like Owl.

It *was* Owl! He was reading out stories he had written about his life. When his friends told him about Eeyore's missing tail, he came up with an idea.

"We write a notice promising a large something to anyone who finds a tail for Eeyore," Owl declared. And off he flew to ask Christopher Robin to write some signs.

Everyone gathered at Christopher Robin's house. Even though the signs were misspelled, the friends understood that this was a meeting about A Very Important Thing to Do.

Christopher Robin called for a contest to find Eeyore a new tail. The winner would get a special prize – a yummy pot of honey.

Pooh and his tummy couldn't wait to get started. Soon, Pooh found the perfect tail for Eeyore. It was his very own Pooh-koo clock. It worked quite nicely until Eeyore sat down.

CRUNCH!

Next, Piglet gave Eeyore his own friend B'loon for a tail. That did not work either.

Soon, everyone came forward to present Eeyore with some kind of new tail. But none of them felt as right as his old one.

Finally, Eeyore tried Kanga's scarf. He was quite happy with his new tail. Kanga felt the same way about her honeypot prize.

Meanwhile, Pooh's tummy would simply not let him rest from his honey search. He came across a piece of yarn lying on the ground. He followed it right to Eeyore.

But Eeyore was unaware that he was dragging something along with him.

Pooh tried to warn him, but he was knocked right off his feet!

Pooh's tummy then led him to Christopher Robin's house where they hoped to find some honey. But Christopher Robin was not home. Pooh looked down and saw a strange note on the doorstep. He decided to show the note to Owl.

“Let me see,” said Owl. “There’s never been a note written that I could not decipher.”

The note said, *‘Gone out, busy Backson. Signed, Christopher Robin.’*

"Our dear friend Christopher Robin has been captured by a creature called the Backson!" declared Owl.

“What’s a Backson?” asked Roo.

Owl drew a picture of a monster with shaggy fur and horns. He said that the Backson was a thoughtless creature that scribbled in library books, spoiled milk, and put holes in socks.

“It’s malicious, ferocious, and worst of all… terribly busy!” he cried.

Rabbit came up with a plan to rescue Christopher Robin. They would collect things the Backson liked and leave a trail of them leading to a pit. Then, they would trap the Backson in the pit and refuse to let him out until he let Christopher Robin go.

While everyone hurried off to collect Backson things, Pooh and Piglet set off to dig the pit. Pooh supervised while Piglet dug and dug.

Then Piglet and Pooh covered the deep pit with a cloth and used heavy rocks to hold the cloth down. Finally, Piglet placed an empty honeypot in the middle of the cloth – to make the trap look like a picnic.

Meanwhile, Tigger had decided to catch the Backson on his own. When he saw something moving in the woods, he pounced. But it was only Eeyore who had been left behind.

"You and me are going to catch that Backson together!" Tigger cried as he led a plodding Eeyore through the wood.

"Buddy," said Tigger, "if you're gonna pounce, you got to have some bounce. We need to get you Tiggerised!"

Tigger dressed up like a Backson to teach Eeyore how to catch him. But Eeyore had done enough bouncing for one day.

Tigger searched for Eeyore, but he only found his springy, Tigger-like tail. He was afraid that the Backson had struck again and taken Eeyore!

Tigger kept looking for his friend, not realising that Eeyore was hiding – from Tigger!

The rest of the friends walked to the pit to wait for the Backson. Pooh was so hungry, he began seeing an ocean filled with honey and honeypots.

Then, just as suddenly as it had begun, Pooh's honey daydream ended. Instead of splashing around in a sea of honey, he found himself rolling in a puddle of mud!

Pooh cleaned himself off and came upon a real honeypot – in the middle of a picnic setting.

Pooh and his tummy forgot about the trap he and Piglet had set for the Backson. By the time Pooh remembered, it was too late!

HUNNY

When the rest of the friends arrived, they heard noises coming from the pit. They clung together in fear.

"The plan worked!" Rabbit exclaimed. "We caught the Backson!"

But the Backson turned out to be Pooh with an empty honeypot stuck on his head.

Just then, Eeyore arrived wearing an anchor for a tail. Rabbit decided they could use it to rescue Pooh.

Rabbit picked up the anchor while the rest of the group held on to the chain. Then, he threw the anchor into the pit, and all the friends fell in with it… all except Piglet.

Rabbit told a frightened Piglet to go and get the jump rope from Christopher Robin's house.

"All by m-m-my-self?" asked Piglet.

Owl flew out of the pit to give Piglet a speech about courage. Then Owl flew back in, without anyone noticing.

A nervous Piglet made his way into the dark and scary wood. He looked up suddenly to see a red-eyed monster glaring at him from a tree!

Then Piglet realised that he was staring at his friend B'loon. He tugged B'loon free of the branches just as an enormous shadow fell over him.

When Piglet turned, he saw Tigger dressed as the Backson. But he didn't notice the tigger part.

"B-B-B-BACKSON!" Piglet shouted. He grabbed B'loon and ran for his life, with Tigger chasing after them.

Down into the pit they both tumbled.

Just then, Piglet let go of B'loon, who floated out of the pit. "You have to help get us out of here!" Piglet called after him.

While Owl was busy telling everyone a very long story, Pooh looked up and saw the honeypot from Tigger's foot at the edge of the pit. He and his tummy decided it was time to build a letter ladder and climb out to get it.

Back above ground, Pooh examined the honeypot. “Empty,” he sighed as he tossed it over his shoulder.

Down

in

the

pit,

Owl was *still* talking!

THUMP!

The honeypot smacked the top of Owl’s head!

Suddenly, Rabbit noticed Pooh’s letter ladder. “We can get out!” he cried.

Outside the pit, the friends heard a rustling in the bushes!

"Backson!" they cried once more. But it was only Christopher Robin and B'loon.

"How did you escape the Backson?" Rabbit asked him.

"What on earth is a Backson?" asked Christopher Robin.

Owl explained and Pooh showed Christopher Robin the note. Christopher Robin laughed. He explained that he'd written "back soon", not "Backson".

It was all a silly misunderstanding!

Since it was rather late, Christopher Robin suggested they all go home. But first, Rabbit gave B'loon the last honeypot prize for finding Christopher Robin and bringing him to the pit.

Still, Pooh could not rest until his tummy was fed. So, remembering that pot of honey at Owl's house, he went back there and pulled Owl's new bell rope. He stared at the bell rope for a moment, thinking that it looked familiar.

When Owl opened the door, he began to tell Pooh the story of his new bell rope. He had found it just hanging over a thistle bush.

"Nobody seemed to want it," said Owl, "so I brought it home."

"But somebody did want it, Owl," said Pooh. "Eeyore! He was fond of it, you see. Attached to it."

"Oh, yes," said Owl. "Of course, it is Eeyore's tail. I was just keeping it safe for him."

Pooh had to get Eeyore's tail back to him right away. He and his tummy left without even a taste of Owl's honey.

Eeyore tried out his new, 'old' tail. "Seems about the right length. Pink bow's a nice touch. Swishes real good, too," he announced.

That was good enough for Christopher Robin. "Bring out the grand prize!" he shouted.

Pooh had put his friends before his tummy – and won the contest in the end. His prize was an enormous pot of honey!

DRAWN BY ME AND